The Time of Alexander

TTOA

Blake A-L Boyd

authorHOUSE®

AuthorHouse™
1663 Liberty Drive
Bloomington, IN 47403
www.authorhouse.com
Phone: 1 (800) 839-8640

Published by AuthorHouse   12/29/2016

ISBN: 978-1-5246-5779-6 (sc)
ISBN: 978-1-5246-5778-9 (e)

One time many moments

A dice rolls
Time tocks

Grateful for the inspirations for this collection.

Contents

Introduction

I do not wish to waste too much time. Not with my introduction, or in my writing. I appreciate that you have taken the time to open my book. In all that will be shared, in the pages that follow I have done my best to share with you what I believe is most important for now.

The Time of Alexander should be read with attention to the fact that Alexander is a plot device character. A character that may be in attendance, or absent in a story. In a story that Alexander is present you will know this, as his name will be mentioned. In stories that Alexander is absent you will find that you are in an abstraction. Abstractions are artful stories used to shape the overall context of the time's reality.

In all the stories being shared I, the author, am writing to share only a moment in time. The time of Alexander is composed of several moments happen in one time. My goal is to transport you to a place that is familiar in experience, but of my complete construction.

I love writing, and have been writing for years. Writing allows me to explore ideas, and learn through interpretation. I was inspired to write The Time of Alexander by the desire to share something, that may withstand the test of time, with my youngest brother siblings and my nephew Peanut. With that being said you should note that some of the stories may only barely develop before ending. In such a case you can expect for me to pick up on that story in a following volume, or story.

Writing, and releasing a book is a goal that came about recently. I am excited to share with you, The Time of Alexander. Writing, and reading can be a form of escapism. You have the right to take that in any way you wish. For me that statement means that in reading, or writing an individual may go wherever they decide. There is time when we go to the order of external direction. There is time that we go led only by an inclination that something may develop further.

.
.

My goal for you is that you make it to the end of every story being shared. Thank you for your reading, and enjoy The Time of Alexander.

Cheeks & Sunsets

There's a junction; a fork in the road. The indication sign, weathered and strangely pristine, invited progression. "**Left for Validity. Right for Self- Assurance**", the sign remarked on a continuous loop. The sign was unique in that it rested upon an arc base. As it spun it looked like a tongue licking the pathway.

Alexander had walked up on this fork time before. Usually he would then turn around and set back in the direction he had travel from.

Today that was not the case. There was still some anxiety as he took his first steps to the left. *Validity will be important if I am going to develop the esteem necessary for success,* Alexander quietly reasoned to himself. With him, Alexander carried a pocket-sized sketchpad, rophone, one pencil, one pen, and a Zap! headset.

Zaps! are wireless ear plugs that pick up the frequency and waves of music being played within a user-set wave range. Via voice command the wearer can jump through waves, to another, until they found a frequency and wave they like.

As Alexander walked along this path all his environment began to breathe harmoniously. Alexander's shoulders relaxed as he strolled along. He could feel the decrease in atmospheric pressure every so often. The landscape, initially uninteresting, began to transform into a cover of trees and shooting mountain ranges all around. The wind blew a warm breeze along the path to *Validity*.

He tried to see up through the canopy of trees for a glimpse at the peaks of surrounding mountains. A silhouette of jagged, and variously-formed edges was usually most he could get from the shifting views from down low. The environment was stimulating the mind of Alexander in ways not yet experienced. Each breathe of green air brought more clarity to Alexander's mind.

It was hard to tell how far he had been traveling his course. *I've got to make my own way!* For having never traveled down this path Alexander was notably confident in where he was heading.

Onward and forward Alexander continued. Before he knew it, a divot in the surrounding tree line. It was a cozy set up of small wooden structures. Among the structures circling the center of the created space was a place called Cheeks & Sunsets, a bed and breakfast.

The main entrance housed a wall with a beach mural on it. The developer of Cheeks & Sunsets was some young go getter from the West.

Alexander was attracted to Cheeks & Sunsets by the wave his Zap! picked up of Love Train. The place was sharing the track. Inside Alexander found the individuals inside to be a solid bunch. Many of the people were engaging outside of their personal interfaces.

Personal interfaces were introduced by founding partners of the Misanthropic Club. Personal interfaces were packed into a technology no larger than a grain of rice. By way of this technology the interfaces could be placed in any rophone. The interface displayed with direction from the owner's thought waves. From the grain like technology came aesthetically pleasing audiovisual representations of the information sourced from the thought wave. A founder of the Misanthropic Club claimed the innovation behind the technology was a vinyl.

The people occupying Cheeks & Sunsets were smiling, and social.

⋮

"Life is a lot like throwing a party. It could be a bust, even when everyone you invited shows."

Alexander was sitting on a bench with some new-found acquaintances. They were now sharing their opinions on random matters of life. The bunch were not the shy type, to say the least.

"I've always held the desire to throw the grandest party with all the different people I know. I figured I would be doing everyone a service by providing them with an opportunity to mass interact in a common space. With very little restraint beyond indulging in joy," Germaine shared with the booth of faces.

"You are naïve. Your innocent intent pays little attention to favorable association. Who is to say I care anything about who it is you know. Let alone about who you know. Really, I'd rather be at home, or privately entertaining my own. "The orator of these words, Al, sipped from a flask big enough to hold his mimosa.

"I've got to say I am more inclined to think in line with Al here. A party is more about having the right people. Those right people are usually my people," replied Victor.

"Tick-tock, dead clock! New topic guys. I think we can all agree the matter of accepting an invitation has much to do with the perception of what it is tied to." Durp was sitting on the right of Alexander when she decided to move the group's conversation along.

⋮

Alexander was awake in enough time to see the sun break through the landscape at its knees. He stuck around to grab a sausage, egg, bacon, and cheese croissant, with an Americana. Many of the people he had shared time with last night were from Validity.

As Alexander set out back on his journey of discovery he considered the impressions from last night's company. He pumped up his *WALKERS*. Off the porch of Cheeks and Sunsets he headed into the direction of Self- Assurance. Alexander felt certain that he possessed all the necessary tools to forge his own path, 13 miles, to Pluto Hall -the epicenter of individual pursuit in Self- Assurance.

Pluto Hall.

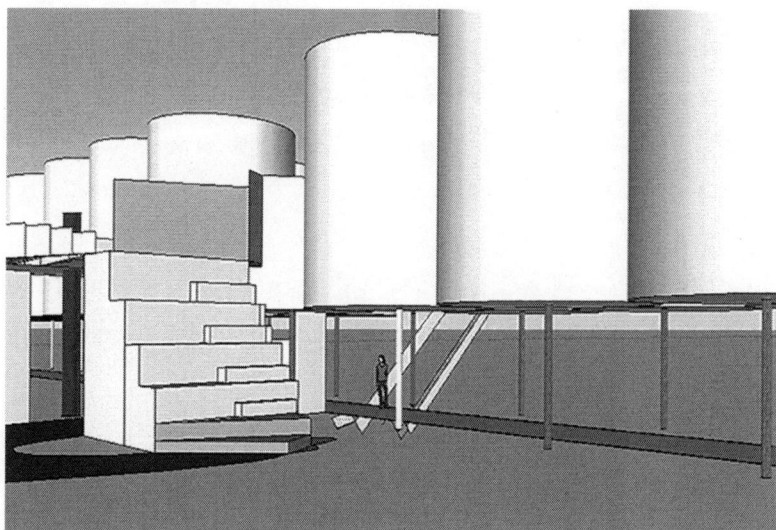

Morning After

"We are not like the rest of them, we are brothers. We have common ideals. Tonight, we are having fun though," Bo mentioned in passing. The *lituation* awaiting show to be no different than the usual, on outset. The members of House of Options [HOO]lived a supreme life. As life progressed members of HOO could expect life to continue on in a positive trajectory. The members of HOO could best be described as cosmopolitan. HOO's were a flock of folk that you'd see on the street alone, then shortly develop a certainty that this person belonged to a greater whole.

On this day Alexander and his fellow *HOOsians* were planning to put on privately, with a selected number of friends. The setup would not be unlike the ordinary. Members of the House of Options had year-round access to their house. Members could come, and go as freely as they wished. Time was like the views from the balcony at the House of Options, rolling continuously, nearly uninterrupted.

The atmosphere at the House of Options was a tri-blend of playground meets physical education, meets office space. The sort of cordial environment prevalent there made it a favorable place for personal development and learning. Members are chosen.

.
.

"That girl isn't ugly, she just doesn't know how to dress." Khush was the type to shoot it to you straight. She wore elegant articles of clothing that captured her day to day mood. People that know her know this. Khush had no favorite color, and she liked to dance.

"ha-ha-ha" the company of people cajoled.

"what's so funny," Khush asked, "I'm being honest."

Khush grew up in a place where the peoples style sense is as barren as the soil they lived on. She became noticed on a standard application for her captivating combination of articles, in her youth.

At the time of meeting Alexander, she was amid transition to a new territory in self-expression.

"Oh cut it Khush, not even the finest of polyester could save her," spouted Britney. Khush's friend Britney came dressed in red on this night.

"Speaking of polyester checkout my new souvenir t, pure steez," remarked Khush.

"Ayyyy-yo!" Someone was coming down the hallway with a swell of energy. It was Bo. "What y'all doing?!"

"Oh Bo, have you met Britney yet?" Khush asked.

"Yep, I'm doing it right now." No sooner than Bo and Britney get to mingling a commotion from the door's other side.

"Maybe we should go make sure everything is all right," Alexander suggest. The party makes a move out the door, down the hallway, and outside the House of Options.

⋮

"I'm feeling **big**, and drunk tonight y'all!" Said a figure from across the pathway from HOO. "Looks like you HOOsians are having a good ole time, privately entertaining tonight. If it weren't for the cars outside, I'd probably never guessed anyone was home."

The remark was backhanded. Alexander and Bo couldn't have cared less. Both were too lit for that shi. Both knew how important it was to keep a low-profile during private entertainment occasions. If too many people found out, then they'd all end up feeling hurt that they weren't invited. The headache of explaining wasn't always worth it for the members of HOO.

It was initially unclear to Bo, and Alexander just who the foreign figure across the way was. The figure then began to move toward the party of individuals: Caldwell, Bo, Alexander, Khush, Sam, and Britney. Open and closed door-time were generally well enforced during private entertainment occasions.

Guests of HOO private entertainment occasions knew that they were to show up to the house by the time the doors shut, or they would not be allowed in at all. Company of the House of Options were free to use the balcony still, during the time.

Bo, Alexander, and their guest had broken the seal by opening the door in the first place. During the exchange between the outdoor parties this prior was all forgotten.

C-Patrol was known to stroll the pathways at night, in an effort to control the ruckus. That was enough to keep most people of the time in door after 9 o'clock. It was after midnight at the time of engagement.

"You lowly pneumatic thot," said the shortest of the figures as they moved into the light.

"Aye watch your mouth when you're in the presence of HOOsians, and their guests, gee," Alexander shot.

"I do what I want," said the speaking figure. It was now beginning to take on familiar characteristics to Alexander.

There was an exchanging of words between the individuals outside HOO.

Things got a little physical between Caldwell, and the foreign figure later identified as Lurch. Lurch refused to leave the property of HOO as requested by the HOOs, and before you knew it Caldwell's time sensitive gasket blew.

Alexander saw an opportunity to cool matters down, and stepped in to lay the altercation to rest. Caldwell and Lurch drove each other to peak. That's where each parted. Not before Alexander could confide to Lurch that it was not in the interest of anyone to further escalate the situation between the two groups. When Lurch finally left, Alexander had a feeling matters were de-fused.

Once back inside Alexander, Bo, Khush, and Britney continued where they had left off in spirits. By all accounts the night was rich, and one for the books. Aside from the slip with Lurch and his friend earlier in the night things were smooth rolling. Inside the House of Options persons in attendance cycled through the various quarters of the house.

As the night wound down Alexander walked out Khush and Britney to their vehicles. It was normal for HOOsians to ensure the safe arrival of their guests to their vehicles. As Alexander was saying "ciao!" to Khush and Britney, Lurch is pulling up again.

There was a moment of shock in Alexander's mind. He couldn't believe what he was witnessing. "Ay guy what are you doing back here?" Alexander asked.

"I want that Caldwell, and I want him now. I got the homies with me now, too," stated Lurch.

Things escalated.

smaCRACK!

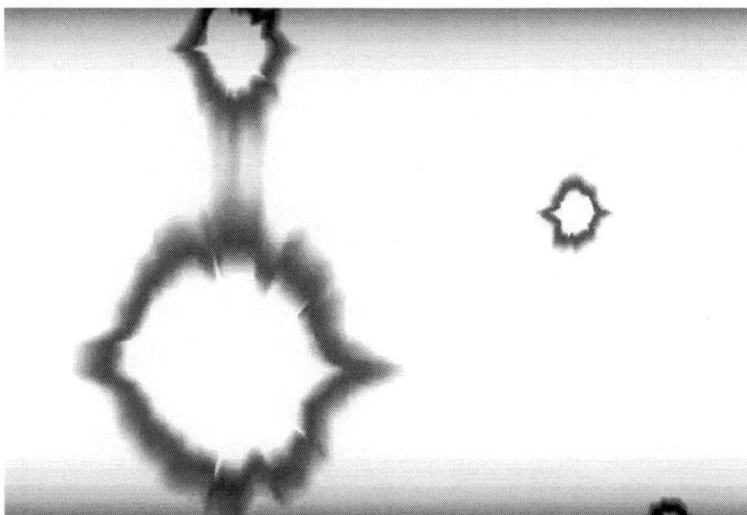

Alexander is semi – conscious in a room that is clinical green. He heard the sniffles come from around he. He could hardly open his eyes.

⠇

Click-click-flash

Flashes of pointed cameras, and blurry figures were before Alexander's eyes.

"Excuse me sir, can you tell us what happened?" a person to Alexander's left pressed.

"Where am I?" Alexander replied – the words barely escaping his tongue.

"You're in the-."

Alexander was out.

Observation

There he sat at Gate 64, hours from departure. As he glanced across the asphalt lot where jets were being taxied in out, he contemplated. The act of contemplation was not new by now. For weeks, he had been taking stock of himself, and his circle.

Long ago Alexander had told his mother he sought to be the caretaker of his family. Life had progressed in such a way over the past few years, that the once naïve remark was beginning to become likely and viable. This was the driving motive behind Alexander's bullish persistence.

All progress did not come without it costs, and misunderstandings. At dinner, a well hydrated *compeer* took shot at Alexander. "You're still in university! What are you doing with your life? At your age, I was getting a raise." These statements had fumed from the belly of Stuey, into the sphere of the quaint tavern. The occasion was meant to be a celebratory reunion of two university pals. The table they sat at would remain occupied by an untouched entrée of wagyu steak after the bunch vacated.

It would be encounters of this sort that Alexander would later cite as renewable source of motivation. Alexander was no stranger to the ways in which others' insecurities would become ammo for attacks on he. This encounter with Stuey made Alexander think back to a talk he once had.

⋮

"I got there when I wanted, everyone thought I was late." A sip was then taken from the chalice at her left. "Could there be anything more ridiculous than time."

⋮

As he sat at Gate 64 on vacation Alexander planned how he would allocate his energy the next 90 days. Alexander's plans were smart and served as benchmark in accomplishing his vision. *What is urgent?* He thought to himself.

This season Alexander was excited at the prospect of accomplishing something he had yet to accomplish before. Right before boarding his plane back to Bankland, Alexander decided that the summer would be largely devoted to improving his understanding of others. To accomplish that he figured he'd spend time people-watching.

Once back in Bankland Alexander got straight to it. He chose a corner off the square to occupy. He sat down, stayed for a while, then decided to head home. Later that night he thought to share his time off the square with his company.

⋮

"I nearly pooped myself. I thought I had it in me to make it all the way back here. I made it maybe 11 blocks, before I could take no more. Because I had sat there too long, peering from behind those iron bars.

If anyone would've asked I would've told 'em it was for the fries. I never took a step into the brick- and-mortar establishment. I sat just outside, eyes in the direction of the setting sun. My eyes remained below the dark green brim of my cap, as I peered through my perfectly sized aviators." Now pulling at the wicks of his mustache Alexander shuffled across the room.

"Not only was my mind pacing, but I was searching. What for? Myself. As I looked at the subjects passing by and those surrounding me, I assessed. Looking for myself in their distance apart, their strides, and even their style.

I asked myself mostly questions beginning with why and what. Exactly what I asked is not important. How I asked is though. I asked by listening." By now everyone was drifting away, half listening, and half deep into a standard interface.

"So I got up!" He suddenly dropped the object he was holding in his left hand. The object had a familiar crack that immediately caught the attention of his party. Relaxed, he continued, "Nowhere was I to be found in those people. What I read in them today made me realize, the questions I'd want to be asked by someone. As well as consider what I would want my outer shell to imply to the seeing mind."

By this time, now satisfied, he began to bop as he made strides. "Truth be told; it was probably the sauce," Alexander remarked.

The party chuckled.

"Yeah ma-an. You know what they say," said a member of the flock.

"Too much sauce, and you'll be lost," several individuals in attendance said simultaneously.

⁘

[observe.DEUX]

Strangely, it's true. It's true that they would rather see you without. See you without your smile, your jewels, and your choins. It doesn't make much sense, but you only need enough choins to keep spending. Strangely it's true.

"Only so little of what's outside ever makes itself in," Theodore remarked. "Of all the ways to change make a couple towards the truth. It's true that things won't always make sense, but always confidence works like glue. I ain't tryna take you to school. You can't afford what I do."

People don't change as much as their paradigms shift Alexander began to realize. The popular don't set precedent. The respected & feared do much more to mobilize a reformation of routine. Once upon a time, to live drunk -no one thought anything of it. It may be ok to reason that maybe no one knew better. *"To know better, is to know different, and that is the true temptation of man,"* said god.

The encounter with Theodore inspired Alexander to write the following observation regarding a norm of his time.

⋮

I've often thought to myself what if the Bible and story of Christ were nothing more than the story of man himself, told in a form which would preserve and preserve the trials of time. In every man/woman is a Christ. The story of an individual that suffers and persists in selflessness for the elevation in knowing our own might.

However, it is undoubtedly true that that many are unwilling to go through the suffering necessary for elevation of not only a positive cause, but of themselves. Many become traitors of themselves, and are turned off by the first experience of hardship. What is new it seems may be discomforting, because we know little to nothing to form a meaning. Christ be those that link together the perceivable symbols to develop meaning.

God is a force. An internal stimulus. In Christ we have a story of an individual that gave his life, the ultimate sacrifice in a selfish world, to become a higher person. That is not to say he had no self-interest in fulfilling his purpose. A problem may be that many don't see themselves in most of the gods[esses], they worship.

"I ask that the authorities relinquish me. That it is seen that I've put to good use the lessons harvested from my trials. Then I pray that the arms for all times be raised, and be as a shield to my posterity, in that they may begin their quest in life upon the foundation for them."

-A Prayer, 2015

Delivery

There seemed to be a prayer for everything, except that which was being sought now. How could one be delivered from themselves? How this situation came about, was in and of itself the result of a delivery. The words that had been running so uncontrollably, in Alexander's youth, were now nowhere to be found.

When things got to this point it was a custom for Alexander to look to the stars. That's just what he did.

"God laughs as we plan," Prett mentioned.

Both he, and Alexander knew that it was in the planning that the vision was revealed. The statement was oddly placed, but relevant to the life both lived.

"Patience," Prett now advocated. Prett knew that Alexander was the type that would much rather laugh with the gods than be stuck in a perpetual state of planning. The two were sitting outside on the patio of their adobe-style quarters. At once Alexander got up.

Now strolling Alexander began skimming through his memory's catalog. *Motion creates emotions, which leads to revelation.* It was a quirky theory, but it oft showed to be true. So he continued to stroll along. His mind was still foggy from last night's celebration of The Slim's life.

The tequila got me, Alexander murmured to himself. He was just beginning to think of how much he was his father's son, when the matter of delivery came back to the fore.

Deliveries were sought-out revelations. A spark. An ah- hah. It was never very clear how long it would take for the delivery to show. There were however learned ways to accelerate its surfacing. Early on Alexander realized a correlation between his looking to the stars for an answer, and the reception of such. He would later build upon this initial realization. Beyond all the *jigging*, what Alexander believed most was that it is in the mind that deliveries are received. These deliveries unveiled truth.

Alexander returned to the place from which he had decided to go. Steady was the chair he sat upon. His return signaled the presence of his delivery. He had just needed to hear himself think. That delivery he sought was verbiage to some, sauce to others, and just what he had been lost in finding shortly before.

CLICK-CLICK-CLICK

the typewriter sang.

⋮

"I just wanted to make some money," the young slick advanced. "Boy did I get that, and more. You see at that time the hood hadn't yet gone to shit. We were still a neighborhood of connected individuals. However, the common thirst for greenbacks began to pry apart the seams of our neighborhood's fabrique." The young slick took some time to collect himself.

"You know there actually used to be streetlights. Now there are just posts for cameras, viewed by the nearest department."

.
.

The Misanthropic Society had asked Alexander to share a time that he shared an alternative approach to solving a problem. The moment he planned to share was one of notable importance to him. Growing up in Frankley presented Alexander with many examples of how to overcome adversity. None were as powerful to him than his decision to live a contrary life. He took to taking principles and lifestyle traits from the likes of those that lived throughout Frankley -as opposed to just those from his neighborhood or skin tone.

At a young age, he showed great potential in being a Block Broker. This early light enabled him to travel throughout all parts of the Greater Napton Area. What Alexander had learned during his time away from his mother's front door crystalized itself once in an unforeseeable manner. This time came racing back to him as he sat transferring it to paper.

.
.

"It began with the old heads, and the young whippersnappers like myself. Some of us sold, other of us consumed. In short, all the opportunity we had was what we could see. The schools had budgets lower than most b-list films. So, in fact, our ability to see was little better than that through a morning's dense fog before sunrise," the young slick continued.

Those words made me think of the schools that to this day have band classes, but the students never got the opportunity to play an instrument. Not once. I refocused on the young slick that was continuing.

"What I am saying joe is we couldn't see. But we could see the rims, we could see the dea-boys dipped in gold. Not to mention our stomach's acid was eating through our spines." The young slick laughed, "Ahaha! Why you think my eyes like this. I had to make choices. Eat, be eaten, or die. Well I ate as you might have guessed. You see what I've felt is the same thing these youngins out hea dealing with today. How will you be able to penetrate the physical with dem words, and views you spend so much time crafting. Choin talks you know!"

This chance interaction showed to me just the significance I may hold in bringing up my community. I met the young slick on the corner of Prep & Post Rd. He stood about 5'2", his hair like a microphone, and his skin chocolate as the river in Willy Wonka's factory. The realities of life had touched his innocence, and corrupted them. There was little direction beyond what he saw. His eyes were strong, off-white, and spent most of the time scanning my features.

To his inquiry, I replied, "I don't have all the answers. But I do have options. Let me put you on something. Present day a good ounce will run you about 250 choins. That's about 9 choins a gram, if the plug ain't your friend. Each gram's market value is 10-20 choins, you do the math on the margins. Or with that same 250 choins you can buy yourself 38 blank t-shirts. That's about 7 choins per tee. Throw something slick on it, and you can sell it for 25 choins plus.

If access for both materials are constant, your risk today with one is outstanding, the other is only personal. Utilize your creativity, and leverage your life experience to get your demand up. If you've made it out here this long, I'm confident you'll be able to figure it out.

There are many ways to eat, slick. I'm not here to save you, I'm here to tell you you've got to save yourself. For those hungry beyond ration I offer the material of my experiences. For those searching for options I have affirmation that deliveries are real."

I felt so proud of myself for sharing this with a young slick. I felt empathy for his position. I suppose I felt I had accomplished something great, just for the mere fact that I had found an alternative way to eat. I must admit I was hoping to pop open a gate that night. The gate of this young slick's mind. Was I successful? Maybe time will tell.

I'll leave with you, the Social Executives of the Misanthropic Society. It is what the young slick shared with me that made this moment so memorable.

*We stood at the corner of Prep & Post Rd. I wore a bucket hat embroidered with cheese not change on a choin graphic. The sun sitting just southwest of noon, in the sky. The young slick was dressed in a crisp bleached tee that shared the sequence of text, "**Now Independently Getting Goals Accomplished**". He looked me in the eyes, and said.*

"I'm just trying to come up. I appreciate the jewels you've dropped, but what I know is what I got. What I got is what I love. I ain't ever going to change what's feeding me currently, for something that might. Keep doing you. You either do it for your health, or you do it for someone else's wealth."

The young slick and I dapped elbows, and went our separate ways.

⋮

Alexander left the paper in the typewriter. He then got up

Born

Alexander was born in a place where the *dea*-boys ride around on rims so big you've got to use a tape measure to measure their diameter, a yard stick just won't do. The women walk if they need to, some to get somewhere and some to give a little self. Individuals' public school experience, during the time of Alexander, was often indicative of a seeming predicted fate.

There were more liquor stores, than gas stations and coffee shops combined. Many people were decidedly mechanical in their ways. The most admirable people still went to the church, but to a lesser extent than in past time. As time progressed it became less of a norm for people to openly worship. Still, any newly developed church was conveniently located just a couple blocks from the liquor store.

The story goes that every Sunday the men would be so *skullied* they'd have to go to church to wash their pores. Through co-operation the women, feeling tired from all the "I'm sorry" these men would stumble in preaching, made it so that the liquor stores were closed every Sunday. At the height of their cooperation the liquor stores were not only closed on Sundays, but open only until noon on Saturday before closing for the weekend.

Because of this weekly capping of the pump **the** *plug* was born.

The name of Alexander's birthplace is Frankley of Greater Napton Area. Frankley, a place of enchantment and infinite possibilities had many people that shared in struggle, but varied in experiences. Frankley was mostly characterized by its formal statutes that made it a friendly environment for those who liked to sleep rather than think. The people of the area were apt to spend time climbing for fun. The closer to Frankley's downtown you got the more likely you were to find the people enjoying themselves through urban interfaces.

Church, liquor stores, and coffee shops largely composed the explorable dimensions of the urban interface, when Alexander was born. It had been only a short time ago that these were the only explorable interfaces that the people had. Alexander was born at just the right hour to be a part of a shift in time. Environments were changing.

Songs were once thought to be the surest way to capture the mind of the people. Eventually someone realized that private interests were using the airwaves to undermine the integrity of the ghetto kids, often referred to as young slicks –if they were male. Many people throughout Frankley began to develop a deafness towards non- Misanthropic Club sponsored audio. This revelation would eventually lead to the Battle of Nigga (BoN).

Sports first began to gain traction as being a culture glue during the time of Alexander. The competitive landscape was just beginning to be dominated by the likes of the Misanthropic Club's two prominent franchises, the Poolsiders and the Courtsiders. Alexander was 13 when he first began to gain awareness of his cultural condition.

.
.

"You probably never would've been born," Zaetoven said. "We can't put back the pieces, agreements have made it so, that to do so would never be in our best interest," he continued.

"I think we've covered our scorn, and accepted things as they are, torn. We don't have to get along," Alexander replied.

Zaetoven, and Alexander were riding on public transit #7. The words shared between the two made Alexander feel cold. It wasn't that the logic of the words felt odd; it was just how true the statements felt. It made Alexander think back to a time of similar feeling.

⁝

"I sit back, and I wonder." Alexander was procrastinating starting on homework for the night, and was instead *caking* with a *tinderoni* from his hall at school.

"How could someone ever settle for less?" It was the first-time Alexander could recall sharing himself so freely. Allee was raking her mind for kind ways to hint at her discomfort of the subject.

Alexander was, now, an open faucet, "How could she love those that beat her…."

"Do you like country music?" Allee injected into the discussion.

"I think she's yet to find what love is," Alexander finished.

"There's this song by Daruckus. The song is about how loneliness is usually thrown around as some form of condemnation. The moral of the song is that you'll be better off loving yourself. I love that kind of country, don't you?" Allee paused for Alexander's response.

"Why won't you love me," Alexander returned. "Aren't I worth it? I'm nice to you."

Allee goofily replied, "you're cute." She was doing her best to seem unbothered. "You're lacking in love and it shows, man. I like you, but I think you like me way more than I like you."

There was a silence.

He hadn't considered that.

"Plus, my father would kill me if he found out. He's not racist, he's just really protective," Anette followed up. "I gotta go, I'll see you around Alexander."

Alexander felt dull as he sat trying to put together what had just happened. In the midst of the positive interactions and lengthy *rophone* sessions, Alexander had thought he'd found something everlasting. It was a loaded situation for him.

•

As Alexander sat there he thought to ask Zaetoven what he thought it would take to positively overcome their differences. The Poolsiders and the Courtsiders lived only 1 stop from each other. Most Poolsiders had an average 10,000 *choins* they could physically touch at any given time.

Many Courtsiders were known to have enormous amounts of unaccounted for time. What an outsider would have to understand is that these fragile differences meant a great deal.

The greater number of choins someone had on Grade Day the better the grade of wings they could afford. People were being *murked* over the grade of their wings now. Wings made people feel like something other than themselves.

The experiences in the place where Alexander was born motivated him to touch the top of the sky, without having to die. It had been nearly done by a Courtsider. The holograms on individuals rophones replayed clips of Poolsiders accomplishing it.

Share a picture with the book cover, and use the hashtag on #TTOA.

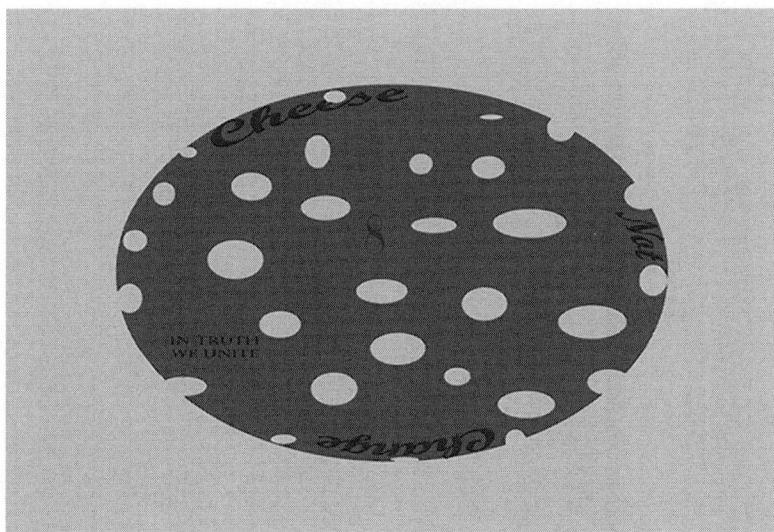

8 valued *choin*. Currency of Alexander's time.

The Misanthropic Club hosts an annual Grade Day in which people from across Greater Napton compete in sky games that test ability & agility. This is the view from a Sky Stop + Gym.

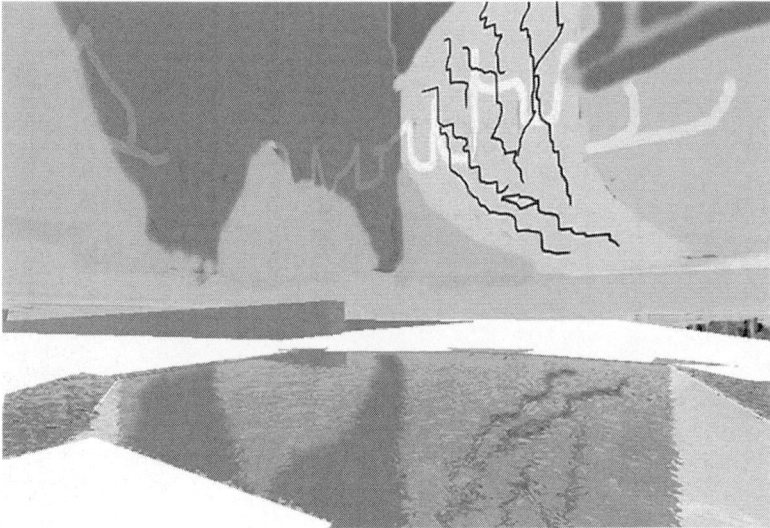

In the Misanthropic Club's Grade Day sky games, some competitors compete in the Gold Flower challenge. The objective is to touch the gold flower in the sky, and land safely. The golden flower is sacred to the people of Alexander's time, and is visible on cloudy days, when even the sun doesn't shine.

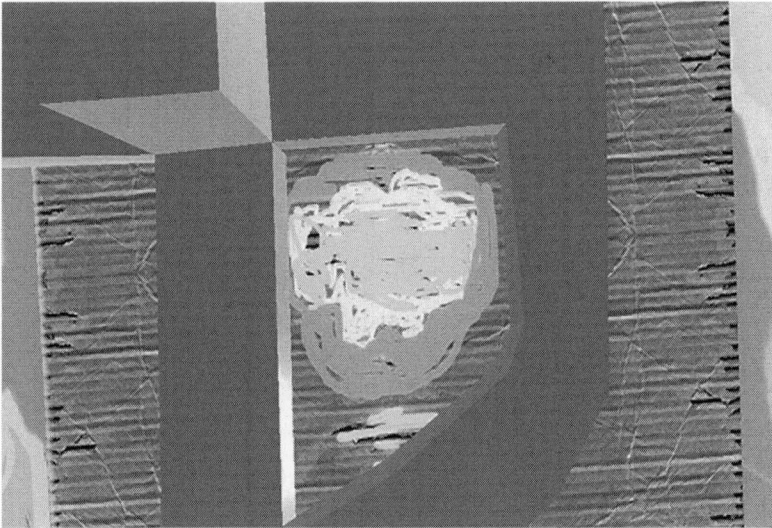

The Misanthropic Club's official Shield

Glossary of Terms

Dea-boys: individuals that engage in risky activities in order to make a profit.

Skullied: the state of being drunk beyond reasonable doubt.

Plug: an individual that assists one, or many in attaining a desired need.

Explorable: Structures, landscapes, and landmarks known and utilized by a peoples.

Caking: the act of blatant flirtation to the point of neglecting things of more importance.

Tinderoni: He/she whom is an object of an individual's affection and desire.

Rophone: a handless communications device capable of projecting holographic visuals.

Choin: a hybrid digital-physical currency utilized during the time of Alexander.

Jigging: A popular dance on Frankley's Far Eastside.

Misanthropic Club: a governing entity that regulated the social lives of the global population during Alexander's time.

Misanthropic Society: a special executive committee of the Misanthropic Club that oversaw philanthropic endeavors.

Murked: To be laid to peace.

Poolsiders: 1 of 13 franchises of the Misanthropic Club that was characterized by its members' access and use of choins.

Private Entertain Occasion: Invite-only affairs, marked by increased door patrol at the House of Options.

Courtsiders: 1 of 13 franchises of the Misanthropic Club that was characterized by is autonomous use of time.

Block Broker: one that engages in the facilitating of the purchasing and transferring of ownership of town & city blocks, plus their residents.

Compeer: a person of equal rank, status, or ability. (Google)

Lituation: a very exciting situation.

Steez: impeccable style.

Zap!: radio wave reader that plays what is on a given wave, and operates hands-free.

WALKERS™: trendsetter shoes made specifically for stylish walking.

Again, thank you so much for picking up my book. I am 24 years old at the time of writing this. Currently I am an undergraduate student-entrepreneur at Indiana University – Bloomington. I would love to hear about your experience with this first volume of short stories. I can be contacted directly on snapchat @dynastyBlake, instagram @7auvage, and twitter @dynstayBlake.